Quiet in the Garden

Quiet in the Garden

written and illustrated by ALIKI

GREENWILLOW BOOKS, *An Imprint of* HarperCollins*Publishers*

for
Lucas
my inspiration

Quiet in the Garden
Copyright © 2009 by Aliki
All rights reserved. Manufactured in China.
www.harpercollinschildrens.com

Watercolors, crayons, and ink were used to prepare the full-color art.
The text type is Cantoria SemiBold.

Library of Congress Cataloging-in-Publication Data

Aliki.
Quiet in the garden / written and illustrated by Aliki.
p. cm.
"Greenwillow Books."
Summary: Sitting quietly in his garden, a little boy observes the eating habits of birds, bugs,
butterflies, and other small animals. Includes instructions on how to make your own garden
and a detailed illustration of plants typically found in a garden.
ISBN 978-0-06-155207-6 (trade bdg.) — ISBN 978-0-06-155208-3 (lib. bdg.)
[1. Gardens—Fiction. 2. Animals—Food—Fiction.] I. Title.
PZ7.A397Qu 2009   [E]—dc22   2008012641

First Edition 10 9 8 7 6 5 4 3 2 1

 Greenwillow Books

I love to go out in the garden.
I see flowers, bushes, berries, trees,
and a little pond.

I sit quietly.
If I am very still, I see more.

I am so quiet, I even hear sounds around me—
chirp, squeak, crunch.
I can almost hear a butterfly flutter by.
I sit still and listen.

Today a robin flew down and
nibbled red berries from a bush.

Why did you do that?
asked a snail.

I was hungry,
said the robin,
and off it flew.

The snail ate holes in some leaves.

Why did you do that?
asked a butterfly.

*It's what I do
when I'm hungry,*
said the snail
as it slid away.

The butterfly sipped
nectar from the flowers.

Why did you do that?
asked a worm.

I was thirsty,
said the butterfly.
And it is so tasty and sweet.

The worm squiggled in the soil to eat bits
of plants and bugs.

Why did you do that?
asked a squirrel.

I was hungry,
said the worm,
squiggling under again.
Good-bye.

The squirrel crunched on an acorn.

Why did you do that?
asked a spider.

Ah-wa-wan-gwy,
said the squirrel,
crunching away.

The spider caught a fly in its web.

Oops, said a turtle.

Well, I am hungry too, said the spider as it ate the fly.

I watched the turtle munch
on soft moss by a rock.

Why did you do that?
asked a lizard.

I was hungry,
said the turtle.
Mmm, mmm, mmmm.

The lizard crawled along a wall
and snapped up a moth.

Why did you do that?
asked a frog.

I was hungry,
said the lizard,
*and I couldn't wait
until dinnertime.*

The frog hopped up and caught a gnat.

Why did you do that?
asked a fish.

I was hungry, said the frog,
and I didn't want to eat you.

The fish nibbled some algae.

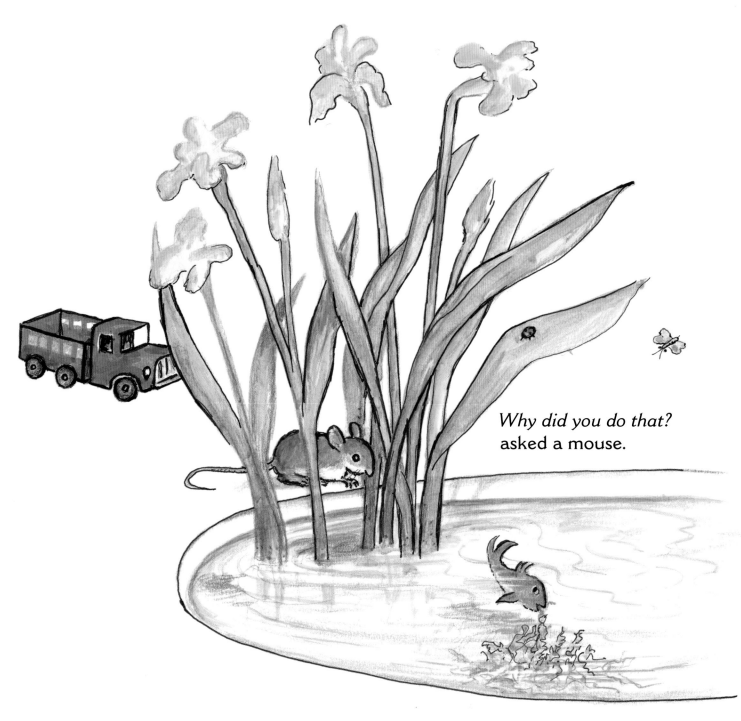

Why did you do that?
asked a mouse.

I was hungry,
said the fish,
and it dove for more.

The mouse crunched seeds, leaves, berries, and bugs in the compost heap.

Why did you do that?
asked my rabbit.

*I was very, **very** hungry,*
said the mouse,
chomping on an apple core.
And I still am.

My rabbit nibbled on a leaf.

"I know why you did that," I said.
My rabbit didn't say, it just munched away.

I picked apples, berries, radishes,
carrots, a cucumber, and more
for a picnic with my friends . . .

the robin, snail, butterfly, worm,
   the squirrel, spider, turtle, lizard,
      the frog, fish, mouse, and my rabbit.

What a racket they all made!
Buzz, nibble, chomp, chew, crunch,
bite, sip, slurp, gulp, swallow, munch.

We were hungry in the yummy,
not-so-quiet garden—
with food enough for all.

Make Your Own Quiet Garden

A garden can be
a flowerpot

a window box

or a patch of soil.

Sprinkle seeds

dig in a plant

or a cutting from a friend.

  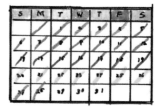

Water every day.

Wait.

Wait some more.

The sun will
warm the soil.

The water will make
things sprout.

Your garden will grow.

Birds, bugs, butterflies, and
other guests will find your garden.
They will be happy you planted it.
So will you.